MW00776263

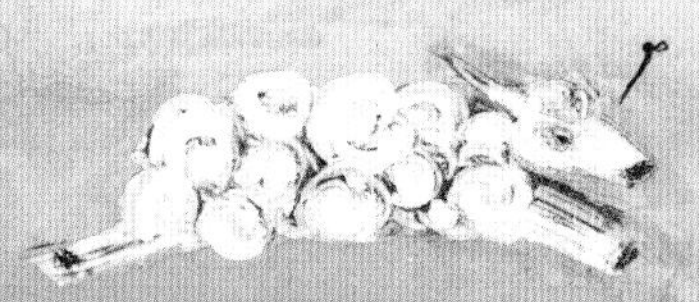

For Gail

Viking
Published by Penguin Group
Penguin Young Readers Group, 345 Hudson Street, New York, New York 10014, U.S.A.
Penguin Books Ltd, 80 Strand, London WC2R 0RL, England
Penguin Books Australia Ltd, 250 Camberwell Road, Camberwell, Victoria 3124, Australia
Penguin Books Canada Ltd, 10 Alcorn Avenue, Toronto, Ontario, Canada M4V 3B2
Penguin Books (N.Z.) Ltd, 182-190 Wairau Road, Auckland 10, New Zealand

First published in 2004 by Viking, a division of Penguin Young Readers Group

1 3 5 7 9 10 8 6 4 2

LIBRARY OF CONGRESS CATALOGING-IN-PUBLICATION DATA
Greenstein, Elaine.
One little lamb / written and illustrated by Elaine Greenstein.
p. cm.
Summary: Describes how a lamb's coat is made into yarn, which is made
into mittens worn by a little girl when she visits the lamb on the farm.
ISBN 0-670-03683-8 (Hardcover)
[1. Wool—Fiction. 2. Sheep—Fiction. 3. Animals—Infancy—Fiction. 4. Mittens—Fiction.] I. Title.
PZ7.G85170n 2004 [E]--dc22 2003019482

Manufactured in China
Set in American Typewriter
Book design by Nancy Brennan

One Little Lamb

By Elaine Greenstein

Viking

one little lamb

lives on a farm

wool is cut

cleaned and combed

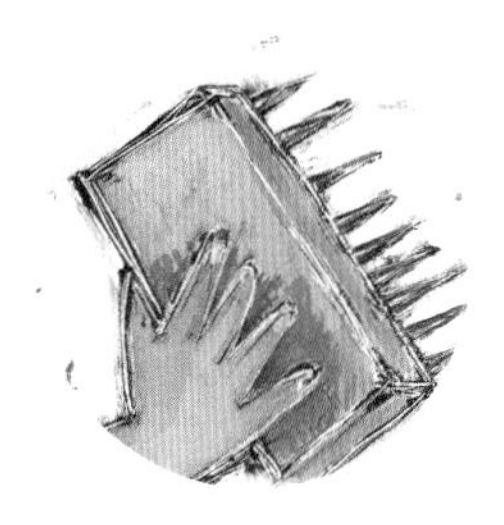

spin into yarn

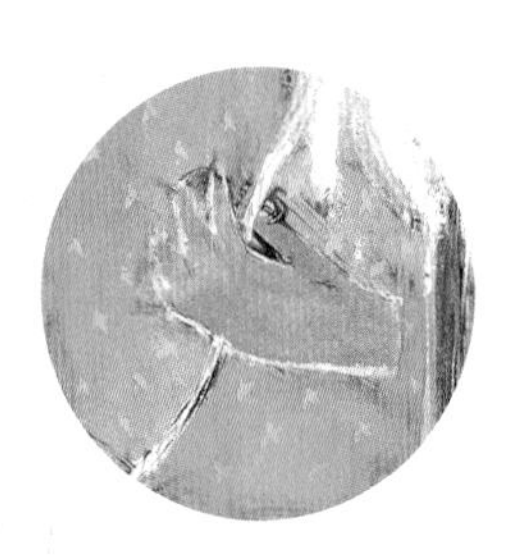

dip into dye

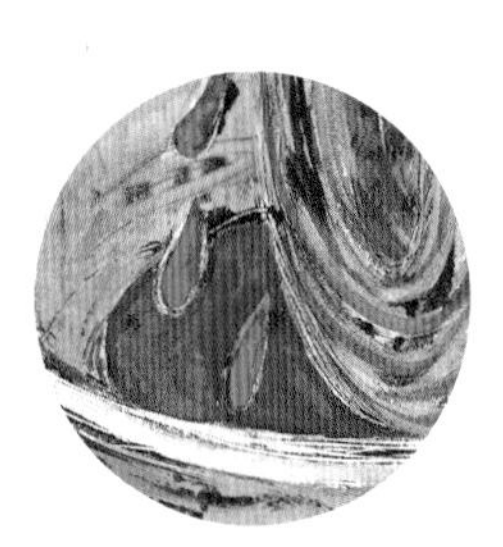

roll into balls

two knitting needles
cast on yarn

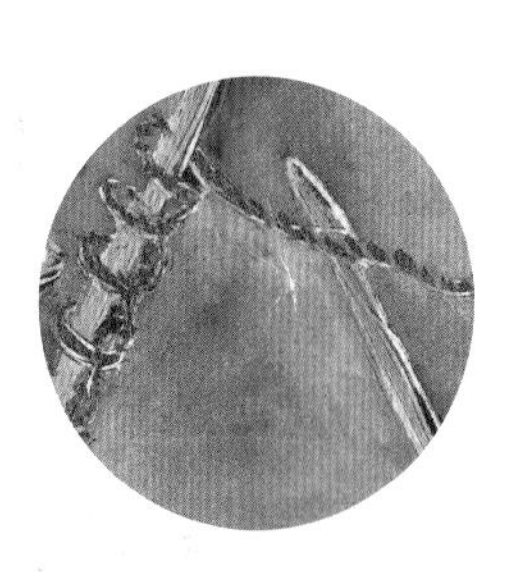

needles between loops
one row then the other

two little mittens
I wear on my hands

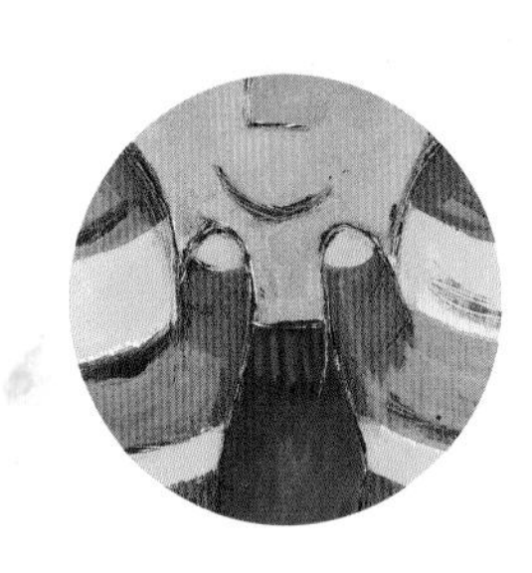

keep my fingers warm

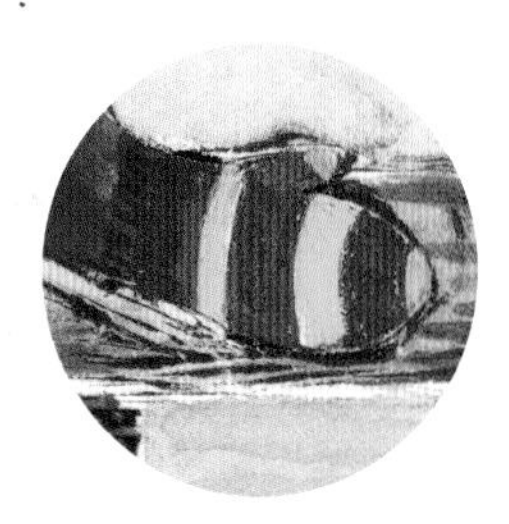

when I visit the lambs